FREYA

KATH LOCK • FRANCES KELLY • CAROL McLEAN-CARR

For Lillian (K.L.)
For my daughters, Gabrielle and Justine (F.K.)

Produced by Martin International Pty Ltd, Australia
Published in association with Era Publications,
220 Grange Road, Flinders Park, SA 5025 Australia

Text © Kath Lock & Frances Kelly, 1995
Illustrations © Carol McLean-Carr, 1995
Design by Steven Woolman
Printed in Hong Kong
First published 1995
First paperback edition 1995

National Library of Australia
Cataloguing-in-Publication Data:
Lock, Kath, 1943-   .
     Freya.

          ISBN 1 86374 203 4.
          ISBN 1 86374 214 X (pbk.).

          1. Mythology, Norse — Juvenile
          literature. I. Kelly, Fran. II. McLean-Carr,
          Carol, 1948-   . III. Title.

398.20948

Available in:

Australia from Era Publications, 220 Grange Road,
Flinders Park, SA 5025

Canada from Vanwell Publishing Ltd, 1 Northrup Cresc.,
PO Box 2131, Stn B, St Catharines, ONT L2M 6P5

New Zealand from Reed Publishing, 39 Rawene Road,
Birkenhead, Auckland 10

Singapore, Malaysia & Brunei from Publishers Marketing
Services Pte Ltd, 10-C Jalan Ampas,
#07-01 Ho Seng Lee Flatted Warehouse, Singapore 1232

United Kingdom (Hardcover) from Ragged Bears Ltd,
Ragged Appleshaw, Andover, Hampshire SP11 9HX;
(Paperback) from Heinemann Educational Publishers,
Halley Court, Jordan Hill, Oxford OX2 8EJ

United States of America (Hardcover) from Publishers Distribution
Services, 6893 Sullivan Road, Grawn, MI 49637
(Paperback) from AUSTRALIAN PRESS™,
c/- Ed-Tex, 15235 Brand Blvd, #A107, Mission Hills CA 91345

FREYA

KATH LOCK • FRANCES KELLY • CAROL McLEAN-CARR

KEYSTONE PICTURE BOOKS

The most beautiful of all Nordic goddesses was Freya, goddess of love and beauty. Her husband, King Odur of Asgard was very handsome and loved Freya as deeply as she loved him

Freya and Odur lived together at Asgard, and both loved beautiful things, but Freya particularly admired magnificent jewels.

Odur loved to travel the countryside and during these times Freya was lonely and unhappy. In her despair she wept. Her tears were as drops of red gold that enriched the ground, and flowers grew wherever she walked.

Near Asgard there was a great hill and inside this hill lived Dvalin and his three brothers, the Dwarfs of Darkness. They were envious of the love shared by Freya and Odur, so they plotted to trap Freya through her love of beautiful things.

They made, from gold and bright jewels, the Brisingamen, the most beautiful necklace ever seen.

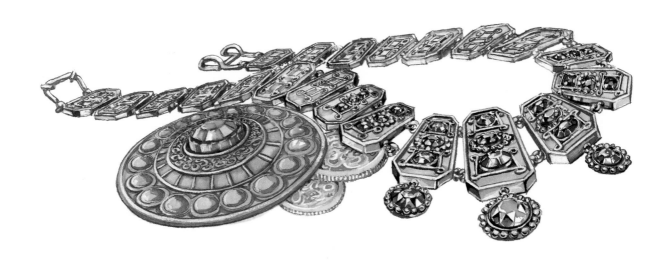

One day, when Odur was away and Freya was walking near the great hill, she heard hammering and voices raised in excitement, so she went to investigate. As she entered their cave, she saw in one corner the shapes of the four brothers huddled over something that seemed to fill the area with brightness.

"This must be the most beautiful work of art we have ever made," said one of the brothers.

"Ah! It is fit for a princess. Even for a goddess," claimed another.

"Any goddess would be proud to own this piece of beauty," said a third.

"Truly, it is perfect," declared the fourth.

Freya ventured closer. When the brothers heard her coming they pretended to be surprised and hid the beautiful necklace behind their backs.

"Are you not Freya, the bride of Odur?" asked the first brother, taking the necklace from behind his back and holding it up so that Freya could easily see its brilliance.

"I am," replied Freya. "And I must ask if you would sell me that necklace, for it is surely the most beautiful work I have ever seen."

"Sell it?" exclaimed Dvalin. "This necklace has no price."

"I would pay well," replied Freya. "If necessary I would exchange all my jewels for it."

"Nothing you have is of such value that it could be exchanged for this wondrous object. Why would we, who can make such an object as this, have need of *your* jewels?" asked Dvalin.

"Well, if you do not want my jewels, I would exchange the flowers which grow where I walk," said Freya.

"We who live inside the earth with jewels of great beauty have no need of flowers," scoffed the dwarfs.

"There must be something you would like in exchange," Freya persisted. "I must have this beautiful necklace and I will pay whatever you ask."

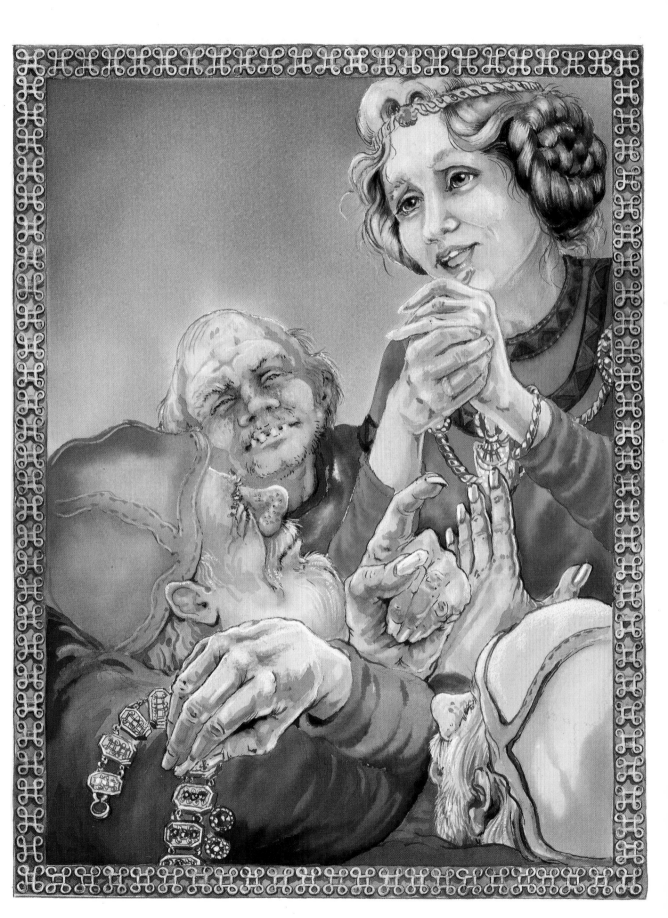

"There is just one thing you could give us," said Dvalin cunningly. "If you allow each of us to embrace you so that we may know we have held the goddess of love in our arms and kissed her, then this necklace can be yours."

For a moment Freya forgot the necklace and she became very angry. "My embrace is for Odur alone," she declared, and turned to leave the cave. However, as she was leaving, she caught another glimpse of the sparkling jewels and her anger disappeared. "Yes, I will do what you ask, for the necklace is exquisite."

So Freya forgot that she was Odur's queen and a goddess and allowed each of the dwarfs to embrace her and to kiss her. In return, the dwarfs gave her the Brisingamen and she departed praying that no one would ever learn of the price she had paid.

But Freya and the dwarfs were not the only ones to know what had happened in the darkness of the cave. Loki, the keeper of fire, and a regular mischief-maker, always seemed to know of such happenings.

Freya returned to her home in Asgard. In her shame and in fear of discovery, she wore the necklace only at night and kept it hidden during daylight hours, but of course, Loki knew her secret.

Eventually the mischief-maker went to Odur and told him of the necklace and of how it had been bought. Odur would not believe him, for he did not doubt Freya's love. However Loki insisted, so the king told him that if it were true, then he, Loki, must steal the necklace from Freya. If Odur were to see it then he would believe him and his heart would break.

"But that will be impossible," cried Loki. "You know how tightly the door of her room fits. I cannot get into that room."

"Then I will not believe what you say," said Odur, "and for your mischief I will have Thor beat you with his hammer."

So Loki planned to bring the necklace to Odur. Being a mischief-maker with an endless supply of cunning tricks, he turned himself into a fly and hid in Freya's room.

That night, when all about him were asleep, Loki flew to Freya's bedside and hovered over the Brisingamen. He saw that the clasp was under her head, so he could not unfasten it. But this did not deter him. He changed himself into a flea, hopped onto Freya's neck and bit her. Freya stirred, turned to lie on her other side, then went back to sleep.

At this instant Loki restored himself to his natural shape. He carefully unclasped the fabulous jewel. Slipping out of the room, the cunning villain immediately showed it to Odur.

Odur was bitterly grieved.

When Freya awoke and saw that the necklace was missing, she knew that her dreadful secret had been discovered. She desperately sought Odur to plead for his forgiveness, but the king had gone.

In her shame and grief Freya went to the great god Odin, threw herself at his feet and confessed to everything.

"I will not rest until I have found him," declared Freya. "I will search for him across the world and beg him to excuse the wrong that I have done."

"And you will be forgiven," said the great god Odin, "but as a mark of your shame you will wear the trinket forever."

Then Odin called for the watchman of Asgard and ordered him to retrieve the necklace from Loki.

So it was that the Brisingamen was brought to Freya, who wore it always as she wandered the world in search of her beloved king, her tears falling as drops of red gold.

That is why, even today, gold is found in many parts of the world as a reminder of Freya's undying love.